ReBoot™

FRISKET TAKES COMMAND

Written by Devra Newberger Speregen
Based on the story,
"In the Belly of the Beast" by Mark Hoffmeier and Lane Raichert

PRICE STERN SLOAN
Los Angeles

Based on the animated series ReBoot™, an Alliance/BLT Production.
Based on characters created by The HUB.
Book Art Direction by Sheena Needham
Book Designed by Michael Sund
ReBoot™ and Copyright © 1995 Mainframe Joint Venture
Published by Price Stern Sloan, Inc.,
A member of The Putnam & Grosset Group, New York, New York.

Library of Congress Catalog Card Number: 95-68051

ISBN 0-8431-3943-9

First Edition
1 3 5 7 9 10 8 6 4 2

In the depths of his Data Dump, at the heart of the high tech metropolis of Mainframe, Old Man Pearson shook violently.

"Let me go, you dumb tin can!" he cried, struggling to break free from his robot captors, Hack and Slash.

"Ah, Mr. Pearson, how very nice to see you again," a raspy British voice said. "Have anything of interest for me?"

Old Man Pearson peered up toward the vidwindow above him. It was Megabyte, Mainframe's most evil virus. Megabyte's goal was to take over Mainframe.

Old Man Pearson snapped, "I said I've got nothing!"

Megabyte motioned to Hack and Slash. "Get me the log," he commanded. Slash found the vidwindow log from a nearby desk and displayed it for Megabyte. Megabyte smiled.

"Well, well . . . here's an old unformat command!" he said. "Really, Mr. Pearson, do you always lie to me?"

"Er, uh, it must have slipped my memory," Old Man Pearson muttered nervously.

Megabyte turned to Hack and Slash. "Go into the dump and retrieve that command!" he ordered.

Hack immediately raced toward the dump with a couple of Megabyte's viral binomes in tow. Slash kept his grip on Old Man Pearson.

"As for our host," Megabyte added, "why don't you show Mr. Pearson how I feel about his dishonesty."

Megabyte then watched the search through his vid-window. "A reward to the one who finds it!" he bellowed impatiently.

Everyone began to dig like crazy. A microsecond later, one of the binomes pulled a small, dimly glowing tetrahedron from the bottom of a junk pile.

"I found it, sir!" the binome cried excitedly.

"Excellent," Megabyte replied. "See if it will still hold a charge."

Hack and Slash rolled up to the unformat command. In a flash, they shot a surge of energy through their cables into the command. It powered up, glowing brightly.

"Full power, sir!" they cried.

Megabyte was pleased. "Bring it to me!" he ordered.

Hack and Slash headed for the ABC vehicle. Suddenly the big jaws of a crane swooped down then snapped shut around them.

"Uh-oh," wailed Hack.

"Hi, trash-diggers!" called a voice.

Inside the scoop, Hack turned to Slash. "That sounds like—"

"—Bob!" Slash cried.

"You got that right, lunkheads!" Bob came from the Super Computer. He had the most memory, power, and RAM a data sprite could have. Bob was Mainframe's hero.

"Get him!" Hack signaled to the other binomes. Soon an ABC full of viral binomes sped after Bob.

Bob zipped around the dump and its compressors on his zipboard. The ABC, on the other hand, ran into one small snag and got squashed flat in a compressor.

Bob turned back to see the ABC pancake and smiled.

On the other side of the dump, Hack and Slash were still trapped inside the crane's metal claws. They struggled to get free.

Below, a mechanical pooch named Frisket watched the crane's scoop swing to and fro. Frisket had been nosing through the junk waiting for his buddy, Enzo, to get out of school.

Just then, Hack lost his grip on the unformat command. It dropped to the ground and landed next to Frisket's front paw. Curious, Frisket gave the command a big sniff.

"Don't touch that!" Hack cried. "Nice doggy . . . HEY!" Before he could say another word, Frisket swallowed the command. The dog licked his chops happily and trotted away to find Enzo.

Back at his headquarters called Silicon Tor, Megabyte watched his vidwindow as Bob freed Old Man Pearson. He felt his insides boil. He glared at the metal piles that were once Hack and Slash.

"An extraordinary performance, gentlemen," sneered Megabyte. "Not only did you let Bob make fools of us, but you let a dog eat my unformat command!"

Hack and Slash both mumbled useless excuses.

"We'll get the dog back," they promised.

Megabyte rolled his eyes impatiently. "Never mind," he muttered. "My way is much better." An evil smile crept across his face. "Get me the boy," he commanded.

Dot Matrix smiled when Bob came into Dot's Diner. But when she got a whiff of the smell on her best friend's clothes, her smile disappeared.

"That smell," she said, "explains the rumor that you turned Hack and Slash into scrap over at the dump."

"Yup. Just giving Megabyte's goons a good reason to leave Old Man Pearson alone," Bob boasted.

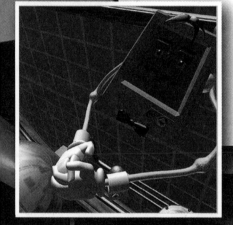

Suddenly there was a commotion behind them. Cecil, the diner's waiter, couldn't believe that a dog was walking through the diner.

"Shoo!" Cecil cried. "You have no reservation! Go on!"

Bob and Dot noticed that there was something strange about Frisket. He was walking funny, and he looked greenish. Suddenly the pathetic puppy collapsed on the diner floor.

Dot nudged Bob. "Go see what's wrong," she said.

Knowing full well he wasn't Frisket's best bud, Bob walked over to the sick hound and gave him a tap. Frisket barely moved. He then checked under Frisket's nose panel hood. Everything seemed normal.

"What's the problem, boy?" Bob asked.

Frisket peered up at him with sad eyes. He opened his mouth, as if to answer. Bob and Dot leaned in closer just as Frisket let out a loud belch—right in their faces.

Dot pinched her nose. "Maybe it's something he ate!" she said.

"Really?" Bob asked sarcastically. "What was your first clue, doctor?"

Reaching over to his other arm, Bob lifted his Glitch from its holder. Glitch was a special tool that could turn itself into whatever mechanical object Bob needed.

"Glitch! Viewerscope!" he commanded. A nanosecond later, Bob held a viewerscope to his eyes and examined Frisket's insides.

"He swallowed an old command," Bob said. "It's trying to unformat his stomach. Glitch! Med-gun!" Bob pointed the med-gun at Frisket's stomach. A pink glow soaked into Frisket's body.

"That's the best I can do," Bob said with a shrug. Frisket's greenish color disappeared. "Maybe Enzo can help him."

Behind them, Cecil was having a fit. "This is not a veterinary hospital!" he cried.

Ignoring Cecil, Dot petted Frisket. "Frisket? Go find Enzo. Go on!"

Frisket came alive at the mention of Enzo. Dot knew how much Frisket loved her younger brother.

With a wag of his tail, Frisket left the diner.

Outside, Frisket searched for Enzo. He heard the familiar sound of a zipboard. "Hey, Frisket!"

Frisket paused before greeting Enzo. He was still feeling sick. He belched loudly again.

"What's wrong, fella, are you not feeling well?" Enzo asked.

Before Frisket could respond, an ABC dropped in silently behind Enzo. Hack and Slash reached out from the back doors and pulled Enzo inside, zipboard and all.

"Let me go, metal-heads!" Enzo cried.

Frisket growled. The ABC's engine roared loudly, ready for take-off, but the vehicle didn't budge. Enzo saw that Frisket's jaws were locked onto the ABC's ramp.

"All right, Frisket!" Enzo cheered. "Sic 'em!"

The back ramp tore loose from the strain, and the ABC shot down the street headed for Megabyte's headquarters, Silicon Tor.

Frisket chased after them.

Outside the Tor, the ABC hovered high above Frisket. Hack and Slash dangled Enzo out the back door, trying to bait the dog.

"Come and get it, puppy!" Hack called out.

Frisket pawed in frustration at the floating ABC. Suddenly a holding pen closed around him and lifted Frisket up to the Tor's roof hatch.

"Hurry!" Megabyte ordered. "We have to get that command out of him before it breaks down any more."

Enzo tried desperately to free himself from Hack and Slash. "Let him go!" Enzo yelled. "I'll erase every last one of you if you hurt him!"

Megabyte appeared and grinned at Enzo. He motioned to his binomes. "Take him to the tank!" he ordered.

Frisket peered nervously out the holding pen's bars. Everyone watched as the pen was slowly lowered into the Tor. "You guys will be sorry you ever messed with *this* boy!" Enzo threatened. "Not to mention his dog!" Just as the words left Enzo's mouth, the pen holding Frisket dropped to the ground with a thud. A crowd of binomes immediately surrounded the pen and began to poke Frisket with electrical sticks, trying to coax him into the tank.

Inside the pen, Frisket lunged at an electrical stick and grabbed it with his teeth. He shook his head violently. The binome on the other end whipped about wildly.

"WHOA!" the binome cried out.

Megabyte sighed impatiently then walked up to the holding pen. "We must move more quickly, gentlemen," he said dryly. With a loud crunch, he pushed the cage with all his might until the cage folded like an accordian.

Frisket was forced inside the tank.

The binome at the control panel activated an energy field. A muzzle and chains locked around Frisket. He struggled to break loose.

"Disobedient as usual," Megabyte said nastily, gently tapping the tank. "Open him," he ordered. "Now!"

A few feet away, Enzo gasped. "Open him? As in operate on him?"

In answer to Enzo's question, a panel on the tank floor slid open, and out came a strange tool of some sort. It hovered over Frisket.

"No!" Enzo screamed, trying desperately to pull away from Hack and Slash.

Megabyte stared at Enzo. "The boy doesn't need to see this," he said coolly. "He's served his purpose. Dump him at the city limits."

Enzo's eyes opened wide. "Can't I at least tell Frisket goodbye?" he pleaded.

"Well . . ." Megabyte said, approaching Enzo. He stared into the boy's hopeful eyes.

"No!" Megabyte finally
replied with an evil grin.
"Stop!" Enzo cried.
"You can't do this!"
Megabyte smiled again.
"I'm sure you'll find something
else to play with," he said,
chuckling cruelly. Then he turned
away and went back to the tank
where Frisket was captured.

Just then, Enzo had an idea. He felt for the yo-yo he always kept strapped to his belt. He smiled. "Yeah," he muttered to himself, "maybe I will find something else to play with."

Megabyte glanced at the file search vidwindow. "Hurry," he ordered. "The signal is growing weak."

A binome stationed at the controls threw another lever. Meanwhile Enzo casually played with his yo-yo, fascinating Hack and Slash, who forgot to guard him.

"Cool!" Hack gushed, as he watched Enzo's yo-yo tricks.

"Up and down, up and down," Slash added. "Hey! Can you do walk-the-dog?"

Enzo smiled innocently, then spun around toward the tank's control panel. "Play with this!" he shouted, flinging his yo-yo at high speed toward the panel. Before the binome at the controls could react, the yo-yo slammed into the levers and deactivated the energy field.

"Containment field off," a computer voice croaked loudly, just as the yo-yo zipped back into Enzo's hand.

"Yes!" he cheered happily.

Inside the tank, Frisket snapped open the shackles and broke off the muzzle. Then he quickly chewed through the tank.

Megabyte threw up his arms and headed for the control panel. "Must I do everything myself?" he barked angrily, grabbing the controls.

But Enzo's yo-yo had completely broken the panel. Quickly Frisket leaped on top of Megabyte and pinned him to the wall of the tank. Hack and Slash let go of Enzo and backed away. That dog was crazy! Without a micromoment to spare, Frisket pulled Enzo onto a nearby elevator platform, and the two descended out of sight.

"What a bunch of dipswitches!" Enzo said with a grin.

Still pinned beneath the tank wall, Megabyte waved his arms furiously. "After them!" he cried angrily. "After them!"

The Tor's long corridors were dark and winding. Enzo and Frisket slowly crept through in search of a way out.

"This way!" Enzo whispered.

Megabyte and his goons suddenly spotted them walking in the distance.

"Cut them off!" Megabyte ordered in a harsh whisper.

Enzo lead Frisket down the hall. "I think we've lost 'em!" he said hopefully. One glance over his shoulder told him he was wrong.

"Uh-oh," Enzo croaked, staring into the robot faces of six binomes. He grabbed Frisket and whirled around, ready to run in the opposite direction. But the binomes had surrounded them, pointing tasers right in their faces.

Frisket let out a small whimper.

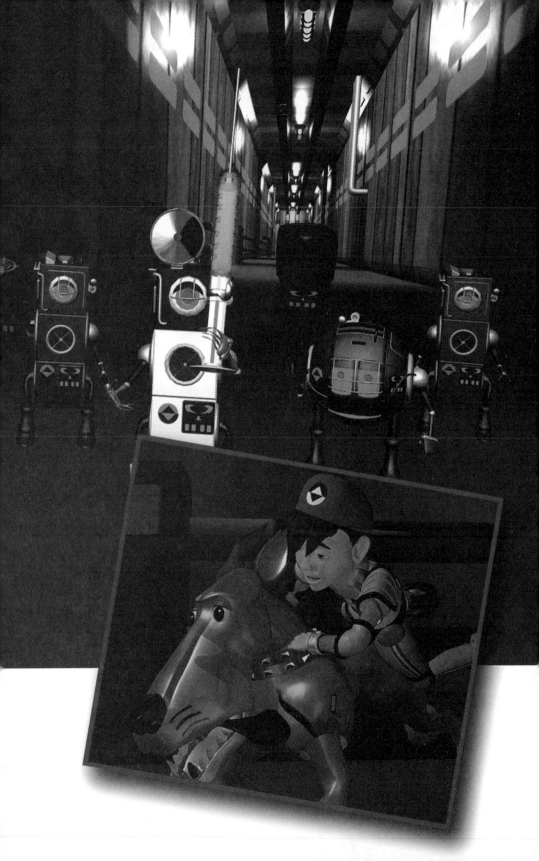

22

Enzo and Frisket stood frozen as the binomes closed in on them. The binomes raised their arms and shot out long cables. The cables wrapped around Enzo and Frisket, tying them together.

Frisket took off down the hall with Enzo tied securely to his side, dragging the binomes behind them.

"Hey!" Enzo cried out with a laugh as they raced down the corridor. Enzo told Frisket to make a sharp right. The binomes and cables separated, flying off in all directions.

After losing the binomes, Enzo and Frisket wandered into the Tor's main Power Room.There, Enzo made Frisket chomp through a power cable. The Tor went dark

"They're at the power controls," Megabyte said. "Activate emergency lighting, then go get them! The binomes raced off. Megabyte rubbed his hands together. "Now we have them!"

"Uh-oh, crowd up ahead!" Enzo cried. He pulled Frisket and ran in the opposite direction. "This way!"

The squad of binomes chased after them. Enzo and Frisket ducked into a huge room filled with amazing weapons.

Enzo gaped around the armory in total awe. "Dude! Look at all this stuff!"

Just then, he heard the metal tapping of steps. The binomes were closing in on them. Frisket leaped up and grabbed the first weapon he could find. He tossed it to Enzo.

"You guys are toast!" Enzo cried.

Before the binomes could retreat, Enzo pulled the trigger. To his surprise, the weapon was a rubber boat launcher! The rubber boat shot through the air and landed on top of the binomes, covering them completely.

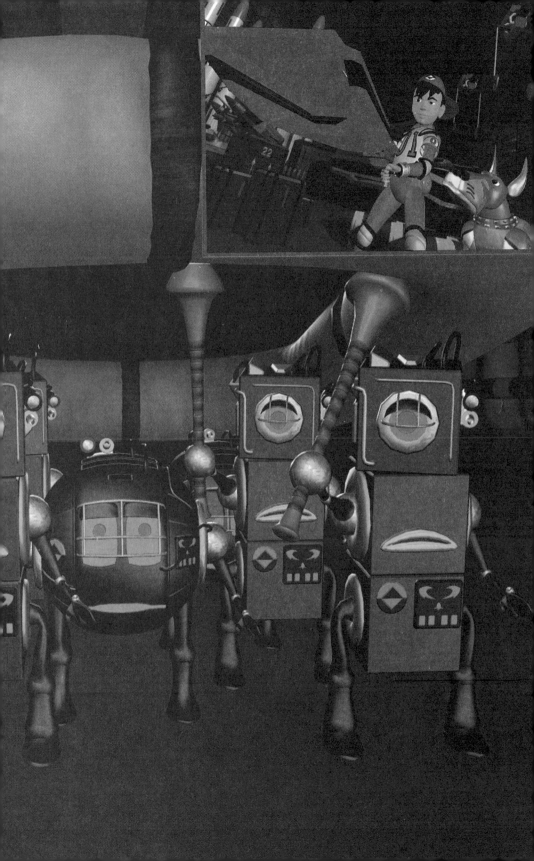

Enzo and Frisket exchanged surprised looks.

Frisket grabbed a rocket launcher and aimed it at the rubber raft. The binomes saw the real rocket launcher pointed at their heads and ran out the door—smack into Megabyte!

Megabyte glared at his goons. "We're not running away now, are we?" he demanded angrily.

"No, boss, no way, nuh-uh, not us," the binomes replied nervously. They ran back into the armory, only to come racing back out a nanosecond later.

This time they were followed by Enzo, who was behind the controls of an ABC, driving wildly after them. The ABC careened into a wall, then smacked right into a rubber raft before taking off down the hall.

"This is too cool, eh, Frisket?" Enzo asked.

Frisket popped out from a nearby hatch and stuck his head and front paws out the ABC window, panting happily into the wind.

Enzo and Frisket sped through the corridors with Megabyte on their tail. Megabyte was fast. He caught up to the ABC and jumped over it, landing in its path. With a mighty power surge, he held out his arm and stopped the ABC head on.

Frisket popped open the escape hatch. He and Enzo bailed out, just as Megabyte lifted the ABC over his head and slammed it into a wall.

"I want my command!" he yelled.

Frisket raced over to an air shaft and ripped off its metal cover with his teeth. Before Enzo could protest, Frisket pushed him down, then turned to face Megabyte.

"GGRRR!" Frisket growled.

Megabyte studied the dog. "Hack! Slash! Where are you?" Hack and Slash appeared immediately, eager to please their leader. But one look at the snarling dog in front of them, and they stepped back.

"Oh," Hack whined. "No, please, Boss!"

"I have a headache," Slash complained.

Megabyte glared at the scaredy duo, then pointed to Frisket. Reluctantly Hack and Slash rolled toward Frisket, who instantaneously reduced them to bits a second time.

"Sorry, boss," the piles of iron whimpered from the floor.

Megabyte sighed in frustration. Frisket escaped down the air shaft after Enzo. They were free!

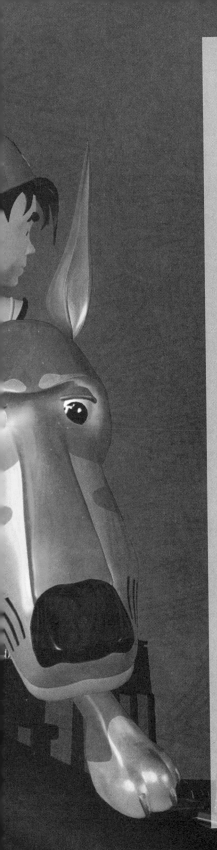

"C'mon, Frisket, what are you waiting for?" he asked.

Frisket stared back at his friend. The green color had returned and his little body shivered.

"Frisket? What is it, boy?" Enzo asked. He stepped closer. Frisket let out a small moan. Enzo made a face and turned away. "Ewwww, Frisket!" he cried. Frisket had just thrown up the command.

Frisket carried Enzo across the crane. "After them!" a voice suddenly called out from below the crane. Megabyte, Hack, and Slash were coming! Enzo grabbed ahold of the crane cable.

"Frisket!" he called out as he jumped from the platform. "Follow me!" Enzo landed on the ground and looked up at his dog. "C'mon, boy!" he called up to Frisket. "Just slide down the cable! Hurry!"

A nanosecond later, the dog was on the ground. Enzo laughed, petting Frisket happily. "You're feeling better, aren't you, boy?"

Frisket barked in reply.

"Let's go back to the diner," said Enzo. "I'm sure Bob and Dot are wondering where we are!"

Back at Silicon Tor, Megabyte found his precious command, but it was not a pretty sight. Hack and Slash were in for it now!

"Enzo! Are you OK?" Dot said when they returned. She looked worried.

"Yeah, we were just coming to save you," Bob added.

Enzo and Frisket stared at them.

"Save us from what?" Enzo asked casually.

"From Megabyte!" Bob cried. "What happened?"

Enzo smiled proudly, then rubbed Frisket behind the ears. "Oh, nothing," he replied with a shrug. "Me and good ol' Frisket here just kicked Megabyte's bitmap. That's all."

Bob and Dot exchanged surprised glances, then Bob bent down to pet Frisket. "Looks like we owe you one, boy."

Frisket growled, and Bob withdrew his hand. "Ah, right, um—good dog!"

Enzo laughed and scratched Frisket behind the ears. "No, GREAT dog!" he corrected.